Ballerina Girl

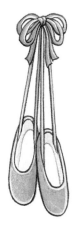

Note

Once a reader can recognize and identify the 34 words used to tell this story, he or she will be able to read successfully the entire book. These 34 words are repeated throughout the story, so that young readers will be able to easily recognize the words and understand their meaning.

The 34 words used in this book are:

a	can	fly	I	on	the	twirl
all	crown	for	I'm	pink	tie	while
ballerina	dance	girl	in	sky	tippy	with
ballet	day	gown	like	spin	toes	you
bows	do	hair	my	star	tutu	

Library of Congress Cataloging-in-Publication Data
Hall, Kirsten
  Ballerina girl / by Kirsten Hall ; illustrated by Michael Koelsch.
    p.   cm — (My first readers)
  Summary: A little girl puts on different costumes and pretends
  she's a ballerina performing for an audience.
    ISBN 0-516-05363-9
    (1. Ballet dancing—Fiction. 2. Imagination—Fiction. 3.
    Stories in rhyme.) I. Koelsch. Michael, ill. II. Title.
III. Series: My first reader.
PZ8.3.H146Bal 1994
(E)—dc20   94-12246
                                                       CIP
                                                       AC

Ballerina Girl

Written by Kirsten Hall   *Illustrated by Michael Koelsch*

CP CHILDRENS PRESS ®
CHICAGO

Text © 1994 Nancy Hall, Inc. Illustrations © Michael Koelsch.
All rights reserved. Published by Childrens Press ®, Inc.
Printed in the United States of America. Published simultaneously in Canada.
Developed by Nancy Hall, Inc. Designed by Antler & Baldwin Design Group.
11 12 13 14 15 16 17 18 19 20 R 02 01 00 99

I'm a ballerina girl.

I can spin. I can twirl.

I can do a dance for you.

Do you like my pink tutu?

I can tie my hair in bows

while I dance on tippy toes!

I can dance! I can fly!

Ballerina in the sky!

Ballerina in a gown.

Ballerina with a crown.

I can dance for you all day.

I'm the star in my ballet!

I can spin. I can twirl.

I'm a ballerina girl.

About the Author

Kirsten Hall was born in New York City. While she was still in high school, she published her first book for children, **Bunny, Bunny**. Since then, she has written and published ten other children's books. Currently, Hall attends Connecticut College in New London, Connecticut, where she studies art, French, creative writing, and child development. She is not yet sure what her plans for the future will be—except that they will definitely include continuing to write for children.

About the Illustrator

Michael Koelsch has lived most of his life in Huntington Beach, California. He loves to take advantage of the wonderful weather year-round and enjoys participating in dicathalons, playing soccer, beach volleyball, and roller hockey. He loves all kinds of music, especially reggae, blues, jazz, and classical. Koelsch likes to surf every morning before he sits down to paint.